The
Last Speck
of the
World

Flavia Idà

Dedication

For my grandson Benjamin

Acknowledgements

Thanks to Steven Radecki for his spot-on edits,
and for prompting me to write this story.

Thanks to Niki Lenhart for another beautiful cover.

ONE

A NOTHER NIGHT when the world seemed so beautiful she could almost be persuaded it was the work of creators. The full moon hung in the cloudless sky, dripping silver on the black expanse of the sea, and the pine trees stood tall under a crowd of stars. If the world was the work of creators, she wondered, had they created it because they were lonely?

Illuminated only by the red pulses of the beacon arcing up from her front steps, she could see the shapes of the houses rising next to hers along the bluff, no light in any window. She owned all of those houses. Were she so inclined, she could have spent every day in a different one.

Every house had its charms, every owner had made her a bequest. The owners of the house around the corner had left her a handmade quilt, those of the house next to the kindergarten a full spice cabinet, those of the house opposite the post office a grand piano. She could not use all the bequests, but they were all hers for the taking. She was the wealthiest woman in town.

How quiet the world had become. No more car horns, no more bird calls, no more children's laughter. No more ambulance sirens screeching day and night for miles around.

She switched on her portable music player. Lovely cascading notes, centuries old, filled every corner of the house. Sometimes she kept the music player on all the time. She had no human voices except those of the singers; without them, she would lose her mind.

In a corner of the living room sat blind and mute the television set. No more movies, no more cartoons, no more documentaries, no more nature shows, no more weather reports, no more sports events. No more news. When the world was a full nest, she'd wondered whether by hovering in space one could hear an aural corona around the planet, the incessant buzz and hum of billions of souls and billions of machines talking to each other.

On a corner of the desk sat unused the computer, once king of tools and mighty messenger of the earth. The net wide as the world had no more dots to connect. The only thing the machine was still useful for was keeping a castaway's log.

She'd never felt the desire to keep a log. Among all the endless needs of everyone who ever lived, she needed a sense of purpose. Her only purpose now was to preserve her life; chronicling day in and day out the diminished, tiresome tasks she had to perform in order to preserve her life seemed a waste of time. And who would read her log?

She was familiar with stories of castaways marooned on desert islands; everyone was. Humans, exquisitely social animals, had been fascinated by the speculation of what they would have done if they had been deprived of each other's company.

One story told of a sailor who was the sole survivor of a shipwreck; another told of a young girl who was the sole survivor of a massacre. Both had endured long enough to be rescued, after a number of years. She could have never imagined that she would be a castaway on a desert island encompassing the planet.

But if she ever decided to write a log, she knew what the first entry would sound like:

I am female, thirty-two years of age. I live in the last speck of the world, on a bluff above a barren sea. My name is not important. There is no one to call me by my name. My race is not important. There are no longer races. My nationality is not important. There are no longer nations. It is now ten months, three weeks and five days since I was appointed custodian of the planet. All the machines are dead. All the clocks have stopped. I do not know why the plague has spared me. It has taken everyone I loved, everyone I hated and everyone I never met. Not a day goes by when I don't think about ending my life. What keeps me breathing is the hope that perhaps I am not the sole custodian of the planet.

She went to the kitchen, lighted like every room in the house by industrial-strength, motion-activated flashlights she'd screwed to the walls under the ceiling. After she'd remained alone, she'd slipped into the habit of talking to herself.

"Hmmm, do I want to cook tonight? No, not tonight. I'll make a cup of tea and … I'll have some cookies, yes, and some peaches."

From the cupboard she took a can of peaches, and from the cutlery drawer the most important of her kitchen utensils, the can opener. She checked the expiration date on the can: still good for ten months. On the label were two smiling farmers holding full baskets, along with the words "All Natural" and

"Pesticide Free". Not that it made any difference anymore — no farmers, no pesticides, no problem. She hummed the jingle that had made some shoppers want to buy that brand of canned peaches and not another.

She remembered the taste of fresh peaches, their pink fuzzy skin, their sweet juice on her lips. She missed fresh foods — milk in dewy bottles, raw tuna tasting of the ocean, apple pie warm from the oven, ripe tomatoes scented with basil. She missed all fresh life.

Her cutlery and cups were plastic, her plates and bowls were paper. Water was too precious to waste on washing metal, china and glass. Instead, she cleaned her cooking pots by wiping them with paper towels. She used only the kettle, a pot and a pan.

One thing she didn't mind washing was her favorite mug, made of sparkling white porcelain and graced with the gold logo of her alma mater. She'd never been one to get attached to material things, but if she lost the mug she'd be as close to grief as one can be after losing everything else.

The kettle was whistling. She poured hot water into the mug with the teabag in it, put the mug, a spoon, the cookies and the peaches on a tray, and went to sit on the patio.

The moon had dipped in those ten minutes or so. It was no longer above the pine trees but behind them, a bright faraway dot crisscrossed with the mingled black outlines of the branches. If she had spent those ten minutes looking only at the moon, she would have seen it move with her naked eye. My God, she thought, does the earth spin that fast? One could go mad thinking about it.

The tea was fragrant, the peaches not too tin-tasting, the cookies not too stale. She ate and drank slowly, savoring the night breeze, listening to the windchimes and to the sea that never sleeps. Then she went back inside and closed the patio door. She didn't have to worry about dangers from humans or animals, not even a mosquito bite, but the habit still made her feel safer.

She dumped the empty aluminum can, the plastic fork, the paper bowl and the cellophane wrappers into a single trash bag, and put the bag in a trash can by the front door. There was no longer any need for her to sort trash for recycling, but she still used only compostable bags. She hated having to throw away what remained in cans and jars when she didn't finish the contents, but she had no choice; she could neither refrigerate the leftovers nor feed them to animals.

Tomorrow she would cook — perhaps the basmati with saffron her neighbor never got to make. Saffron had been the most expensive spice on the planet; she bought it only as a special treat. Now she could have all the saffron she wanted, but she still used it seldom, so it would not lose its specialness.

Time for bed. Like so many of her days now, she'd spent the day bicycling, walking, pushing, lifting and carrying heavy provisions. The provisions she would need to get tomorrow were lighter, but would require more bicycling and more walking.

In the bathroom, the bathtub she could no longer use was stacked with jugs of bottled water for flushing the toilet, the purest water that ever flushed a toilet. Some of it came from mountain springs halfway across the world.

She cleaned herself with hospital cloths, then toweled off. Bath towels were the one household item made of cloth she still used. She reasoned they were for the drying of a clean face and clean body, so they never got dirty enough to need washing too often.

She opened her medicine cabinet, studiously avoiding the mirror; she wasn't sure she wanted to see the results of having to cut her own hair. In the medicine cabinet she kept a tube of lipstick and a small container of mascara. She no longer used makeup, but she didn't want to throw away the two last items she'd bought.

Only three tablets of the sleep drug left. She'd have to get another month's supply tomorrow without fault. After water and food, the drug was her third highest priority. She'd never needed it before; now she couldn't do without it.

She was grateful for the drug in the same measure as she detested it. Every time she took it, she was reminded that for all intents and purposes she had become an addict. She wouldn't call it medication; no doctor had prescribed it for her. It had been prescribed by whatever it was that had stopped the world and wiped out her peace of mind.

She swallowed the tablet with a sip of water. The drug worked quickly. It spared her the harrowing limbo between the time her mind could no longer stay busy with today and the time it could not yet get busy with tomorrow; the time that ambushed her with the thought of all the things she could not change. She switched off her music player and was soon fast asleep.

Outside, the beacon kept pulsing, as it had done without interruption for ten months, three weeks and five days.

TWO

S HE WOKE UP WHEN SHE NO LONGER NEEDED SLEEP, as she always did now that she was no longer tied down to timetables.

The first thing she did every morning was check the beacon. The beacon alerted her well in advance when the batteries needed to be replaced; the daily ritual was unnecessary, but it comforted her. She put on her slippers and went to open the front door.

From a place she couldn't pinpoint, she heard the sound of a child crying. She hadn't heard the voice of a living human in a very long time, but no one forgets the sound of a child crying. Everything else stopped being important.

She could only guess the direction from where the crying came. She raced up and down the laneway, to the end of the street, all around the house.

"Where are you, where are you?"

Then she saw her: a little girl sobbing in the middle of the road.

"Oh God."

Without even looking at the little girl's face, she was hugging her and crying and panting.

"Where are your parents? Do you have anybody? Are you lost? Are you hurt? What's your name?"

The little girl kept her face downcast, whimpering.

"It's all right, it's all right. You're with me now, you're not alone anymore. I will take care of you, I will keep you safe."

She took the little girl by the hand and started walking toward the house. The small, warm hand held hers tightly. It had been so long since she'd felt a human touch.

She pointed at the house. "Look, see? That's where we're going. You're safe, you're with me now."

Then she felt the small hand slip away from hers. She turned around: the little girl had vanished.

She woke up gasping for breath. It had been one of those too-vivid dreams she knew, the drug's most dangerous side effect. She beat her fist on the nightstand. How she hated the drug. It always found the deepest corner of her pain: she was the little girl, a helpless child trying to soothe herself. The price of sleep was borderline insanity, and she must be able to rely on her mind at all times; there were no other minds she could rely on. When the shock subsided, she reached for her robe and got out of bed.

She slept on the bare mattress, with a blanket but without sheets. She kept the drapes always open and the shades always up: privacy was not important, light was. On the nightstand were the music player, a glass of water and a book she'd started to read some days before. She also used to keep an alarm clock there, that alarm clock she had so hated sometimes.

On the nightstand at the other side of the bed was the upturned glass shade of a lamp that used to be on her desk next to her computer. After the lamp had become useless, she'd unscrewed the basket-like white shade and she'd put in it the collection of small fossils she'd found years earlier during a hike in the mountains.

Still shaking from the dream, she went to check the beacon's batteries. They had eleven months left, but she knew that. She lingered on the threshold, waiting to hear a little girl crying and knowing it was absurd. She returned inside and switched the music player on. The singer's voice, clear as a crystal bell, seemed to come from a regret that was taking too long to heal.

She went to the kitchen and turned on the portable stove. She'd run out of fresh coffee, and made a cup of the instant. She wasn't hungry after that dream that had rattled all of her, but she needed her strength. She took two nutrition bars from the cupboard and put them on the tray, along with the coffee in her white and gold mug.

There had been a time when she ate while watching television. The sofa and the armchair in her living room were still facing the screen, the focal point that for centuries before the machines had belonged to the tribal fire. She finished breakfast while listening to the slow, wistful song. Then she washed the mug with bottled water, letting the water drip into a pan so she could reuse it in some other way, and wiped the mug clean.

Time to inspect her treasure chests. The house was spacious. She and the man she'd been engaged to had bought it four years before, while they were planning a future together. When they'd signed the contract for a house spacious enough for a family, she didn't know that the man she was engaged to was planning a future with someone else. After she'd left him, she'd trashed, donated or sold every smallest thing showing he'd been a part of her life. It was only her house now.

From her desk she took a pen and a notepad embellished with jolly cartoons of produce under the caption *Let's Go Shopping!*. The notepad came from her best friend, who used to joke that the only real necessities of life are toilet paper and chocolate.

She would never run out of the necessities of life. The plague had struck so suddenly, and had killed so quickly, that no one had stockpiled for survival. Everything had remained in the stores, and she'd become the only consumer. She wrote "Coffee" in her *Let's Go Shopping!* list.

First she checked what she used to call her future nursery. It was almost entirely occupied by neatly stacked boxes of batteries of every kind. In a corner were a reserve beacon and a small portable vacuum. A look around told her that in a couple of months she would have to replenish flashlight batteries. She closed the door, on which she'd taped a sheet of paper with the word *Caution* in red marker, to remind herself to tread carefully around that small arsenal of explosives.

Then she checked what she used to call her guest bedroom. It was piled with clothes, shoes, kitchen gear, over-the-counter medications and toiletries. High on a wall was tacked an unframed print of Van Gogh's last painting. She hadn't found a better place for the print; every inch of space in the house had been taken over by mounds of things not meant to be kept in a house all at once. A look around told her she had to replenish paper towels, liquid soap, painkiller and dry shampoo: four more entries in her shopping list.

Last she checked what she used to call her studio. She'd kept her books there, until she'd had to cram them on her two living room bookcases, on the end tables and on the floor. Half of the room was full of bottles and jugs of water, the other half of non-perishable foodstuffs in cans, boxes, bags, wrappers and jars. A look around told her she had to replenish creamer and salt: two more entries in her shopping list.

She closed the third door. Unbelievable how much a single human being needs, she thought. She envied the dead; the dead need nothing.

THREE

S HE GOT DRESSED IN HER BICYCLING GEAR, minus the now unnecessary reflective vest, then went to the garage and opened it by pushing up its heavy door with all her strength, so the door wouldn't roll back on her.

In the garage she kept two top-of-the-line hiking bicycles, the second a brand-new spare. The bicycle she rode was equipped with four large saddlebags, still not enough for what she had to bring home. She'd been thinking for a long time about what she could do to save herself some of the trips; perhaps a lightweight travois, if she could figure out how to make it work. Her brother used to say that naming the problem is half the solution. She'd named the problem, but she hadn't found the solution.

In one of the saddlebags she kept a bicycle pump, a tire repair kit, a large rolled-up piece of tarpaulin, a length of rope and several sturdy net bags. The bicycle had a headlight, but she no longer rode at night in the pitch-dark streets.

She had removed the steel basket behind the seat, and had substituted it with the larger wicker basket where she used to keep newspapers and magazines. When she'd moved the wicker basket to the bicycle, she'd stacked the newspapers and magazines under her desk. She'd read all of them, and every word in them, but she didn't want to throw them away. The last headline on the last newspaper was *God Help Us All*.

She hooked the music player to her belt, tucked in the earpieces, tied her foldaway helmet under her chin and slipped a backpack on her shoulders. It was the backpack she used to take with her when she went hiking; now she took it with her every time she left the house.

In the backpack she kept a powerful flashlight with swiveling beam, a Swiss army knife, a hooded waterproof poncho, a pair of heavy-duty gloves, two pairs of sanitary gloves, a safety mask, a one-liter bottle of water, a thermal aluminum blanket, a box of disinfectant wipes, ten nutrition bars, a bottle of painkiller tablets, one of caffeine pills and one of the sleep drug.

She had put together the backpack so that, if she got stranded far from sources of provisions, she could live off its contents for at least ten days. When she'd gone hiking, she'd also taken her video camera with her; nothing worth recording now. Through the hole in one of the backpack's zippers she'd attached a small plush rabbit, a childhood toy.

It used to be that every time she'd left the house she'd taken with her a purse containing what had been the four essentials of her times: car keys, house keys, pocketbook and cellular phone. Once, she'd lost her purse; gathering back the four essentials had been yet another headache she wouldn't have to worry about again.

She no longer wore a watch. She now measured the hours as they had been measured before humans had allotted them numbers: daytime and nighttime. But calendars were as vital to her as the marks prisoners had scratched on the walls of their cells. Without calendars, time would have melted into an amorphous jumble.

She had a two-year calendar, a very pretty one showing landscapes from various countries, some of which she had hoped to visit. She'd always thought it was an act of faith to buy new calendars without knowing whether one would live long enough to use them; a two-year calendar now seemed like a supreme act of faith.

What no longer mattered was what humans had named the days, and what they had assigned to the days called by that name. It was said that God worked for six and rested on the seventh; she could now work on any and rest on any.

In the garage was also her car, covered with a thick layer of dust. If there had still been spiders, it would have been covered with spiderwebs too. The useless machine took up so much space. The only thing she would have wanted to save, if she could have removed it, was the sticker she had affixed to a corner of the back window: *Ignorance Is The Root Of All Evil.*

Her house was separated from the bluff by an ample front yard adjacent to a wide paved laneway. She could have thrown her trash off the edge of the bluff from there, but she didn't want her house to overlook a garbage dump. She took the trash bag from the can, carried the bag five houses down and tossed the bag off the lawn of a neighbor who'd been a good amateur painter. The non-biodegradables would last forever, but she was the only polluter. Going back on centuries of progress had simplified a great many things.

She glanced at the gazebo crumbling under the pine trees, trying not to think of the parties and cookouts she used to have there with friends and loved ones. At the base of the bluff, the beach was long and smooth: no footprints, no pawprints, no bird tracks. The only sounds were the waves and the wind; but the wind still smelled of wild grass and of the sea. She could not have lived away from the sea, not even now that the sea was a desert.

Her neighborhood had been one of the most sought-after on the coast. Everything now was starting to look like ancient ruins: shaggy trees, falling doors, ivy on the windowpanes, broken things on the stairs. On the wall of a condominium hung a banner showing a group of people happily gathered around their dinner table: "*Now Leasing. Discover luxury living and stunning ocean views!*"

Her speck of the world was the only neat one. She could do nothing about the repairs her house would eventually need — if she lived until then — but she could do something about what surrounded her house.

The trees took care of themselves; she took care of her front yard, her backyard, her hedges and a good stretch of the laneway on both sides. She pruned and fed and weeded, pouring gallons of chemicals. It was back-breaking work, but she loved it. She would not yield to nature's encroachment, not while she had strength to fight it. She mowed the grass using a manual lawnmower with a wooden handlebar that she'd bought years before as a decorative antique. Everything old was new again.

She looked at the sky. The darkening clouds had that mottled look that meant rain. It worried her; rain complicated everything. She mounted her bicycle and set off at a good pace, taking the road that ran along the bluff.

Cars, motorcycles and trucks sat in driveways and in garages left wide open. More vehicles stood in the middle of the road, smashed into each other, and she had to weave around, careful also of the broken glass. On the pavement were the parallel green tracks of the bicycle lanes. She could have never envisioned that someday every yard of asphalt would be a bicycle lane, and she would have everywhere the right of way.

Something else that no longer worried her was road rage. Violence too had found a permanent solution. The world had become as peaceful as humans had always wished it could be, and it had happened when the world had been scoured clean of humans.

She looked at all those abandoned vehicles, whose keys she would never find.

"I should have learned to hotwire," she joked wearily.

The first couple of days after she'd remained alone, she'd driven her car to the closest store to stock up on her first priorities: water, food and batteries. She'd spent hours loading up bottles, bags and boxes one by one, until there was no room left in the car. When the gas tank was almost empty, she'd gone to the houses of her neighbors, found the keys to their cars and brought home more supplies, shuttling back and forth until, one by one, the gas tanks of her neighbors' cars were almost empty. After that, it had been her bicycle and her legs. She was very thankful to her body for having stayed as healthy as it had always been.

Halfway to her destination, she passed the spot where five years earlier a boy of fourteen had been killed in an accident without guilty parties. His loved ones had left a small roadside memorial: a smiling photograph of him and plastic flowers. The photograph would become shreds, the plastic flowers would last. Every time she took the road along the bluff, she saw that reminder of the inanity of life.

She'd almost reached the commercial center. As she pedaled past a car straddling the curb with the front doors open, something caught her eyes. On the passenger seat was a small narrow box in red giftwrap. She dismounted and leaned the bicycle against the car's side.

Next to the gift box was a card showing a mortarboard, a diploma scroll and a bottle of champagne. Inside, in elegant cursive, was the phrase, *"Congratulations, we are so proud of you!"* and the signatures "Mom" and "Dad". The card was very much like the one her parents had given her when she had obtained her advanced degree.

The gesture of ripping gift wrap gave her a stab of pain, as she remembered all the joyful occasions when gifts were opened. Inside the box, nestled in pink velvet, was a beautiful diamond bracelet, the kind she would have loved to wear if she still wore jewelry. It must have cost the parents a good deal of money, money they had loved to spend.

She held the sparkling bracelet in her hands, fighting tears.

"Do I want to think about it?" she whispered. She shook her head. "No. It won't help anybody."

She gently laid the bracelet into its pink velvet coffin and put it back where she'd found it, next to the card. Then she mounted her bicycle and peeled away.

FOUR

THE COMMERCIAL CENTER was named after the sunflower field that had been paved over to build it. It was home to most of what had been the major needs of her times: food store, discount store, drugstore, pet store, tobacco store, automotive store, liquor store, beauty store, restaurants of diverse ethnicities and a branch of the institution that had nourished them all, the bank.

The center had also housed the offices of various professionals: lawyers, chiropractors, dentists, therapists and tax preparers. The tax preparers had prepared her taxes for many years. There used to be a popular saying that the only inevitable things in life are death and taxes; the only inevitable thing in life was now her death.

From the supermarket's doors left partway stuck open wafted a stench of rot. The last time she'd eaten fresh food was two days after she'd remained alone, while the refrigerators and freezers held and the produce hadn't yet spoiled. After that, all perishables had begun to perish, and every store that sold perishables had become a garbage dump without the vermin. When she had to go there, she wore safety masks taken from the hardware store.

Every store, office and restaurant was a dark, dusty cavern. No more ceilings screaming with neon, no more piped-in music, no more crowds of chattering people coming and going with something to do.

At first, out of habit, she'd pushed her shopping cart toward the checkout counters. It had taken her a bit to get used to the idea that she could now bypass every checkout counter in every store. Many of the cash registers had remained open, full of paper and metal.

The easiest store to access was the discount store. It didn't have automated doors, and it didn't sell perishables; no rot or mold there. The discount store had also been called the one-bill store. She'd shopped there often; her salary was adequate but not lavish. The one-bill store was now the no-bill store.

She left the bicycle in the rack, took the flashlight out of her backpack, hung it from her neck and aimed the beam forward. Then she got a cart, walked into the store and took the shopping list out of her pocket.

"So … salt, creamer, coffee, paper towels … What else? There should be room left for paper plates, maybe some cans, too."

She took the items from the shelves and put them in the cart. Every time she went to a store, she had to remind herself to leave out non-essentials that would crowd out the essentials, but she didn't always resist the temptation. She kept promising herself that someday she would go to every store within her reach and take home nothing but non-essentials. Life wasn't only the basics.

She'd always liked scented candles and silk flowers. She hadn't lit a candle since the day she'd remained alone — no fire brigade if she got distracted — but she could have all the silk flowers she wanted. She gathered an armful of orange zinnias, white lilies, pink roses, blue pansies, green bamboo leaves, and a little bird made of *papier-mâché* and real bird feathers.

She rolled the cart out of the store and stuffed her provisions into the bags. She loaded some of the bags in the bicycle's saddlebags and some in the wicker basket, shuffling the contents around to make the most of the space.

Last, she loaded the silk flowers on top of everything in the basket, planting them upright so they wouldn't wilt, and found a nest for the little bird so it wouldn't fly away. She smiled at the thought of riding home with a garden fluttering behind her.

Her final stop was the drugstore. Before going in, she took with her one of the empty bags; only half of the automated door was stuck open, barely enough for one person to pass through. She got a two months' supply of the sleep drug, a bottle of liquid soap, one of dry shampoo, one of painkiller and two boxes of her favorite crackers. While she walked past the pharmacy booth, bare of all medications, she tried not to remember that if she ever needed a prescription, even for simple antibiotics, she was done for. She loaded the rest of her provisions, switched off the flashlight and set out for home.

This time she took a different route, but not the street where the service station was; its underground tanks left unmanned had enough gasoline to set off an explosion. She also tried to avoid passing too close to electricity and telephone poles. Now that no one was maintaining the poles, she worried about being hit if one toppled over. But she no longer worried about being electrocuted; the world had stopped being at the mercy of almighty electricity.

Two years earlier, the town had gone through a massive power outage. It had been ludicrously caused by mice chewing through a cable, and it had lasted an unprecedented six days. She remembered how quickly what they'd called civilization had unraveled in six days.

The outage had happened during an unusually cold winter. They'd slept bundled up in clothes, they'd washed with cold water, and they'd driven around looking for food stores with enough generator power to have stayed open. If there were no open food stores within reasonable distance, they'd driven around looking for open restaurants and cafés, just to get a cup of hot coffee in the morning. They'd used flashlights until the batteries had died, and then candles. Half an apartment block had accidentally been burned down by tenants no longer used to working their way around open flames indoors.

Without electricity to recharge the computers, one couldn't work, couldn't stay in touch with loved ones and friends, couldn't while away the time with entertainment and couldn't keep abreast of the news. What had kept her sane through that temporary nightmare was the same thing that was keeping her sane through this permanent one, the thing she called the single greatest human invention: the printed page.

When electricity had been restored, the town's inhabitants had felt the kind of relief their most remote ape-like ancestors must have felt when they could relight their campfires. But the cliché was true: without machines, people rediscovered each other. She and her friends and neighbors had never spent so much time together, playing games and telling stories.

By the time she was in view of her house, it had begun to drizzle. The sea roared with long breakers, while the branches of the pine trees danced against the ashen clouds. She carried in her bags, as many as she could lug at a time, and distributed them to the storage rooms. Then she heated some canned soup, added a dash of seasonings and ate it in the rocking chair by the window. Strange how a bowl of hot soup could make one feel safe, she thought.

When she was done, she went looking for a crystal vase she hadn't used in a long time. She put it at the center of the dining room table and arranged her silk garden in it. The flowers and branches were delicate and lifelike; she wouldn't have taken them if they had been shoddily made. Last, she perched the little bird atop a zinnia, smiling.

"Aren't you a little beauty?"

She spent the rest of the day reading, while the rain streaked the windowpanes and the wind ruffled the trees. When the last of the light waned, she took the sleep drug, curled up under the blanket and fell asleep to the sound of the sea crashing against the bluff.

The beacon pulsed on in the rainy night.

FIVE

A T FIRST IT SEEMED YET ANOTHER ONE of the new diseases that kept cropping up seemingly overnight from the polluted, battered planet. It didn't take long for the world to understand that this was a scourge unlike any the world had ever seen. It wasn't the sort of danger from which countries could feel protected by their borders; it was the sort of danger that obliterated all borders.

Whatever this thing was, it struck at the core of life itself. One day, everything that breathed began to die. It took even the bodies, and even the bodies of those who died from other causes; they almost immediately crumbled into grey flecks that the wind blew away and the rain dissolved. No one could give it a name. It was simply 'the plague' — the perfect catastrophe.

Her parents lived in a distant city, her brother and his family even farther away. They had exchanged flurries of telephone calls. Would they be safer if they gathered all in one place? And what place would that be, and how would they reach it? Against everything they wanted to do, they had agreed it was best for each to stay where they were for now. She remembered the words "for now" repeated like an incantation, though everyone knew there was no "for now". The last time she'd spoken to her family, her mother had told her, "We love you, darling. Stay strong."

No one knew whether the plague spread through air, water, food, humans or animals. All that could be done was keep away from humans and animals. Most people stayed together, many didn't; many people kept their animals, most didn't. The fabric of the planet was coming undone in a matter of hours.

In the interest of safety, on the first day of the plague her country's head of state, the top members of his cabinet and of the military were whisked away to a shelter in an undisclosed location. From there, they tried to keep the government going, as best as government can be kept going when a nation is dying.

The head of state broadcasted messages, urging the population to help one another and not give up. His words allayed for a few minutes a fear no one had ever felt, even during the world wars. Two days later, all communications from the shelter stopped; the plague had found its way into the place considered the most secure. The end of the broadcasts was the end of hope.

She was on her own. There was no fooling herself that her family would be spared, and there was no fooling herself that she would be spared. It was just a matter of how to pass the time until she too became grey flecks that the wind would blow away. A writer she'd read had said, "Everyone is on death row, time and manner of execution unknown." Everyone now knew time and manner of execution.

She did what everyone did. She locked herself inside the house and waited to die. Two days, three days, four days — barely eating, barely sleeping, barely thinking — while one by one the machines winked out. From between the slats of her lowered blinds, she watched everything that breathed fall down and become grey flecks. The plague from centuries before had reaped a few million humans; this one was reaping them all. Why was it taking so long with her?

On the fourth day, her neighbor of many years knocked at her door, calling her name and begging for help. She didn't know what help she could give him, but she would not let this thing take her humanity too. When she opened the door, the man was already dead at her feet. She slammed the door shut, so she wouldn't see him become grey flecks.

On the seventh day, she awakened from a few hours of fitful sleep to a silence she could almost feel on her skin. She went to the window: the world as far as she could see was covered with grey flecks blowing away on the wind.

She knew she was the only one left. What she didn't know was why.

SIX

A NOTHER MORNING OF WAKING UP to no other sound except the sea crashing against the bluff.

In the past, sometimes she'd used noise-canceling earbuds to block the intrusions of the world — music blaring from a neighbor's backyard, dogs barking in the street. Now she missed even the voices of the machines, the electronic symphony of chimes, jingles, pings, tones, buzzes and chords that had accompanied humankind for the final three centuries of its history.

She went to the bedroom and looked for what she wanted to wear. She'd always been told she had good taste in clothes, but she'd never been particularly interested in the latest fashions, or overly preoccupied with her wardrobe. Now that there was no one to comment on her wardrobe, she had to fight the temptation to give in to frumpiness, to wear the same things until they fell apart.

Her favorite sweater was ripped along the neckline. There was no reason for her to sew it; she would go to the apparel store and get another sweater. Washing clothes consumed water; she took from the stores several items of clothing at once, sometimes two of the same item if she liked it better than others, and threw them away when they became damaged or too dirty. Her apparel, too, had become disposable.

She'd kept the small compulsions she'd always followed before leaving the house: placing the cushions neatly at the opposite ends of the sofa, emptying the wastebasket in the bedroom, straightening the book pile on the coffee table. She didn't know why she felt the need for those repeated gestures; perhaps they gave her the illusion of control.

She walked the bicycle out of the garage, hooked the music player to her belt, tucked in the earpieces, tied her foldaway helmet under her chin, slipped the backpack on her shoulders and started pedaling. The weather had cooled a bit in the last couple of weeks. Winter on the coast was mild, but she dreaded the shorter days, when time dragged on after the light went away so quickly.

What she didn't like about going to the clothing store were the two miles or so where the street climbed to the top section of the town. She used to stop along the way to enjoy the view; now she just pedaled harder.

The town's government buildings rose at the top of the hill. She got off her bicycle and rested for a while on a park bench near what had been City Hall's immaculate lawn, now an expanse of litter and brown grass.

On the roof of the building the flag hung at half-mast. It had been lowered after the first mass deaths, and it had remained at half-mast when it had become clear that it would never again wave from the top of the pole. Across from City Hall stood the burned-out shell of one of the town's oldest houses of worship.

She remembered the faithful gathered inside to pray. The faithful had prayed until the very end.

Even the cemeteries had become useless. All that remained as proof that the planet had once been inhabited by intelligent beings were the things they had left behind: the government buildings and the houses of worship, the schools and the refugee camps, the jails and the museums.

She had reached the clothing store. She leaned the bicycle against the wall, next to the door stuck fully open, turned her flashlight on and went inside, past the detectors that had deterred thieves.

It was a large store, stocked with a wide variety of apparel. She couldn't remember the layout, and had to wander a while until she found the banner: *The Women's Fashions of the Summer Season are HERE!*

"Hah. It's always summer season now."

She made her way to the Women's Knitted Tops and searched for the size Medium section. Halfway down the rack, she found what she was looking for: the same favorite sweater she'd ripped, only brand-new. She put it over her shoulder and headed for the door.

Then she thought she would take something else, perhaps a couple of sweatshirts. She wandered around some more, looking for the Active Wear aisle. The flashlight's beam cast long, distorted shadows that made the mannequins seem almost alive.

Her eyes fell on an item she'd seen in more than one store: a sweatshirt displaying in poorly applied silkscreen the name and flag of her nation. Almost all nations had sold things displaying their name and flag; she found them very curious now. There were no longer nations, no allegiances created simply because someone happened to be born in one speck of the world instead of another. There were no longer wars fought in the name of allegiances gone wrong.

She took the sweatshirt off the hanger, held it against her chest and sashayed down the aisle in a parody of a model on a catwalk.

She chuckled. "This time you're coming with me."

If anyone had asked her why she now wanted the sweatshirt, she couldn't have given a precise answer. Perhaps it was the same as wanting the photograph of a dead relative. She left the store, switched off the flashlight and folded her two new garments into the bicycle basket.

Next to the clothing store was one of her favorite bakeries, its door wide open and its floor littered with trash and broken glass. There was not a corner that didn't bring back the past, and there didn't seem to be any advantage to remembering the past. If it was bad times, she didn't want to revisit them; if it was good times, she didn't want to be reminded that they would never return. Here she remembered the good times when she'd gathered with friends for coffee and pastries, and when she'd bought birthday cakes.

Her birthday had passed over a month earlier, the first birthday since she'd remained alone. She'd spent the day furiously cleaning the house, as if hoping that by wiping things clean she could wipe the pain clean. Every time her birthday fell on a weekday, her colleagues had surprised her at the library with gifts and celebration. She didn't know in what way she would change now that she could no longer interact with people. She knew humans sharpened their character on each other's edges.

The bakery's shelves were bare, except for a few loaves of bread covered with dead mold. So many smells had gone from the world, the pleasant and the unpleasant — freshly-baked bread and exhaust fumes, roses and carrion. Perhaps it was a blessing. Smell was the strongest of the senses. The smallest whiff could open a floodgate of emotions, whether she wanted to feel them or not. Perhaps it was better to have become poorer in this too.

Something small and grey scurried across the floor, making her gasp. She ran into the bakery and chased it around the display cases, behind the counter, into the kitchen.

"Wait, wait, wait, WAIT!"

The small fleeting thing had vanished as quickly as it had appeared.

She held onto a chair. This time she didn't even have the certainty that it had been a dream. Her mind betrayed her; she was losing the one thing that mattered most.

She crumpled on the floor, sobbing.

"Why me? Why am I still here? Why couldn't I have gone with them?"

Her voice echoed in the silence of the dark kitchen.

She felt something cold and flat under her leg. She picked up the shard of glass and held it, knowing how she could use it.

"Do it," she whispered. "Do it already."

Then she put the shard down, wondering again how she'd managed to drag herself from the brink.

After a while, she got up and rode home. She swallowed a tablet of the sleep drug and crawled under the blanket with her clothes on.

By the front door, the beacon pulsed to the sky.

SEVEN

S INCE THE DAY SHE'D REMAINED ALONE, she'd been too
scared to leave her most immediate surroundings. Now, for
the sake of her sanity, it was time to leave them for a while.

She missed traveling by sea, watching the rolling ship slip
away from the land, and she missed traveling by air, feeling the
rumbling airplane break free of gravity's hold. But she didn't
want to live like a wingless insect one more day.

She was ready to go in no time. She would find all her
necessities along the way. Aside from her backpack, the only
items she took were the spare beacon, an extra pair of shoes, a
change of clothes, a swimsuit, some snacks and a book.

It was a history book from her last year in college. She kept
all her old books. When they started to wear out, she wrapped
the covers in butcher paper overlaid with package tape. She was

especially protective of her big books — her dictionaries, thesauri, atlases and encyclopedias. She had neglected them in the time of the machines, when it was faster to run to the microchip than to the printed page. But she knew the printed page would outlast the microchip; and in the end, it had.

Still, the machines had been so helpful. She remembered the awe, almost the affection, she'd felt for the thumping apparatus that had scanned her brain after a bad fall, for that remarkable tool humans had created so they could see into the denser corners of their bodies.

Before leaving, she had a light breakfast of coffee with coconut milk and a packaged croissant she'd left to warm in the sun. She placed the cushions neatly at the opposite ends of the sofa, emptied the wastebasket in the bedroom and straightened the book pile on the coffee table. Then she closed the front door and set out.

It was a beautiful day in late summer. She hadn't made up her mind where she wanted to go. The one place where she couldn't go was any place that hadn't been recently inhabited. There was a time when she yearned to get away from people; that was why she loved hiking alone in the wild.

While she rode around, she found herself at the entrance to the coast road. She remembered that it had been closed to traffic soon after the start of the plague: it was all hers, in one clean stretch. The road followed every twist and turn of the scenic coastline, and had been a favorite of tourists. The freeway running inland over flat terrain was the preferred route of travelers in a hurry; she had all the time in the world.

She rode at a leisurely pace. The only sound was that of the bicycle's tires swishing on the smooth asphalt. The rush of the wind on her face brought back a long-forgotten sense of freedom. It had been wise to take the plunge.

She made only one stop, on the spectacular old bridge that had been on thousands of postcards. She sat on the roadway at the tallest point of the arching span, high above mountains and sea, and enjoyed a snack from her backpack. She could still see the crowds of people snapping photographs of the bridge and talking in a fascinating mixture of tongues.

Later in the afternoon she reached the Blue Cove, a sprawling seaside resort made up of luxurious cottages shaded by broad trees. It was the sort of place she could have never afforded before; she owned it now.

Painted white and blue, the cottages were trimmed with windows resembling large stained-glass portholes. She liked the colors very much; she'd always thought everything built near the sea ought to look like a ship. The topiary hedges on the lawns must have been quite pretty, still recognizable as shapes of bounding dolphins and seabirds on the wing. It pained her that these creatures made of leaves and branches would die, like dolphins and seabirds made of flesh and bone.

First things first: water and food. She hung her flashlight from her neck and headed for the larger cottage that had housed the restaurant. The front door was locked. She went around, found the service entrance open and walked into the kitchen pantry.

It wasn't just any kitchen pantry; it was the kitchen pantry of a luxury resort. Rows of shelves were stocked with expensive delicacies, nothing akin to the stale snacks from the vending machines of hotels she'd stayed at in the past. She would enjoy dining at the Blue Cove.

The drawback was the lack of a portable stove. Each of the cottages had state-of-the-art barbecues in the backyard, but she didn't know what she could cook on a barbecue. One of the best things for an open fire was her favorite food, grilled fish; but better not think about the last time she'd tasted grilled fish. Besides, she was leery of lighting a fire. Taming fire may have turned apes into humans, but she didn't want to play with something this particular human hadn't used in a long time.

Next, accommodations. The door of the cottage nearest to the restaurant was closed, but unlocked. Inside, the spacious and tastefully appointed suite had been left clean and ready for the next guest. The furniture was covered with dust, but nothing that couldn't be remedied.

She took off her backpack and opened the windows. The view was lovely. Along the coast were scattered small islands and craggy rocks capped by evergreens. To the south was the cove for which the hotel had been named, shaped like a perfect half-moon and dotted with natural arches.

The beach was a wide ribbon of pristine pink sand, joined to each cottage by winding cobblestone paths. Everything she needed was there. She took the beacon out of her backpack, turned it on and left it on the ground by the front door of her cottage.

Now for dinner. She returned to the restaurant's pantry and got one of the room-service carts. She took her time putting her meal together. She wanted a taste of every delicacy she could find, from her own country and from other countries of the world: black caviar, *pâté de foie gras*, preserved quail eggs, roast beef in aspic, dolmades, mochi cakes, quince jelly, lychees in syrup, apple butter with cloves, white chocolate truffles.

The server would no doubt have been appalled at her not choosing a wine to go with dinner. She would have had to explain politely that she didn't drink. Champagne was the caviar's expected companion, but warm champagne seemed like an outrage. She chose instead a bottle of mineral water and a smaller bottle of her favorite soft drink.

From the dinner-service table she took two crystal glasses, two engraved bowls, one silver-plated knife, fork, spoon and teaspoon, a pair of lacquered chopsticks, three gilt-rimmed plates embellished with the hotel's monogram and a white cotton napkin rolled inside a napkin ring shaped like a nautilus shell.

"That's what I call living."

She opened the door leading from the kitchen to the restaurant and peeked in. The restaurant was vast and opulent, left in perfect order for the next crowd of diners. She could almost see them, seated under the beautiful paintings of old sailing vessels that adorned the walls. The only indication that diners hadn't sat in the Blue Cove restaurant in a very long time were the dead flowers of the centerpieces.

She pushed the cart to her cottage. After wiping the tabletop clean, she placed on it the cans, jars, boxes, bottles and bags, and arranged the cutlery, chopsticks, glasses, napkin, bowls and plates. Then she took her Swiss army knife and one by one, ceremonially, opened the cans, jars, boxes, bottles and bags. She put portions of the savory foods on one plate, and portions of the sweet foods on another plate. She turned on her music player and sat down to her feast.

From the open windows came the gentle sound of the waves, and music made the world livable simply by being in it. She ate slowly, savoring every bite, relishing even the clink of glass and china that she had lost to her cheap plastic. She didn't know whether she would ever have another meal like this one; she had one now, and the now was all.

When she was finished, she cleared the table, put everything on the cart and left the cart by the restaurant's back door. She took a long walk on the beach, read from her book, washed up and went to bed. The food was delicious, the bed was comfortable and the bedsheets were clean. Sometimes that's all a human being needs, she thought.

EIGHT

S HE WOKE UP AT AN HOUR SHE DIDN'T KNOW and she didn't care to know, from a restful sleep without dreams.

The first thing she did was check the beacon by the door of the cottage. She had no reason to fear that the beacon had failed, but it felt good to observe the ritual here too.

Without a portable stove, she couldn't make hot coffee. She took instead a caffeine pill with her breakfast: a nutrition bar and corn flakes with honey and condensed milk. Her plan for the day was to sunbathe, go swimming, have lunch, read, listen to music, sunbathe again, go swimming again, have dinner, sleep. Today there would be no hunting for provisions, no carrying loads, no bicycling, no cooking and no cleaning. She no longer needed to earn a salary, but she still needed to spend a few days worrying about nothing.

She took her sunglasses and three of the velvety bath towels from the bathroom. As she was about to put on her swimsuit, it occurred to her that she didn't have to wear a swimsuit, or any other garment. She tossed the swimsuit on the unmade bed, chuckling.

"Lucy the hominid minus the pelt."

It occurred to her also that she didn't have to make the bed. Tonight she would simply move to another clean cottage.

The shimmering sand was deep and unspoiled, dotted with shells, bits of colored glass, coral branches and polished pebbles. She picked up a few of each and put them in her sunhat. She'd found shells, bits of colored glass, coral branches and polished pebbles on the beach below her house, but she wanted some from this beach. She didn't know anybody who'd never felt the desire to pick up those small sea treasures and take them home.

She also picked up a silky white feather, long enough to have belonged perhaps to a seagull or an albatross. It wasn't as shriveled as it would have been if it had sat on the beach for a long time, but she couldn't tell whether it had come from a living bird.

The long walk had given her an appetite. She returned to her cottage, took some snacks from the pantry and ate on the luxurious blue and white lawn chair, under the shade of a palm tree.

Just behind the resort, separated only by the coast road, was a cluster of pretty houses painted in pretty colors and sheltered by fine trees, the sort of neighborhood where rich people had lived. The first time she'd seen it, she'd told herself it was best to ignore it. Now, without stopping to wonder whether she would regret it, on the spur of the moment she made up her mind. First she got dressed, as if she were going visiting.

She crossed the coast road and started wandering among the houses. The grass on the lawns was not too tall, the cars were neatly lined up along the curbs and the front doors were closed, as if the inhabitants had simply decided to pack up and leave. It was the prettiest ghost town she'd ever seen.

She didn't know what she was looking for, while she strolled under the fine trees of that neighborhood without a name. She felt a strong pull to go inside one of those houses, although she didn't need anything from a house. Maybe, she thought, she needed the company of ghosts. One thing she knew: she would not go inside a house with signs that children had lived in it, like toys on the stairs or a tricycle by the driveway.

At the end of a winding street was a house that attracted her more than others. Perhaps it was the dormer; her room in her parents' house had a dormer. On the mat was a cheery "Welcome!", and the potted cactuses by the side of the steps were healthy. She loved cactuses; they survived everything.

She stood facing the door with the polished brass knocker, trying to decide whether she wanted to open it. Then quietly, almost surreptitiously, she turned the doorknob. From just this side of the threshold, she looked for signs of children: none she could see. She stepped in and began walking around the rooms.

It was a charming, immaculately kept house. She could tell it had belonged to people who loved it. They had furnished and decorated it beautifully, and they had taken good care of it. They were still there, grouped in framed photographs dimmed with dust.

A handsome young couple, from their first day in the world to their last days in the world, before the world had stopped: the day they had been born, the day they had taken their first steps, the day they had started school, the day they had finished school, the day they had met, the day they had first dined together, the day they had wed, the day they had bought the house. Each photograph was accompanied by names, places, dates, dedications, cards, drawings. Next to the photographs were objects the people in this house had cherished, and small gifts they had exchanged. They had taken good care of their lives too.

In her adolescence she'd sometimes entertained the thought of writing a book, but then she'd always let it go. It seemed too high an ambition; she was too young, she didn't know much about the world. She'd always thought the only way she could write something worth reading was if she could become invisible. If she could see unseen and hear unheard, she wouldn't have to approximate, to invent; she could learn the truth about the lives of people.

A bittersweet smile came to her lips.

"You're invisible," she murmured. "You can write a book about the lives of these people."

The sound of a clock chiming made her jump. Five cadenced strokes boomed in the silence of the house and of the world outside. She'd seen enough. Time to go.

She closed the door and crossed the coast road back to her cottage, leaving behind the pretty ghost town. She got her dinner from the restaurant's pantry — another array of foods she hadn't tasted in a long time and perhaps would never taste again, to be savored to the fullest. The sand was warm, and the rippling waves lapped gently her bare feet. She remembered the pelicans that used to fly north at that time of the year, the first bird and the last bird in the flock constantly changing places.

Then she looked for another clean cottage, and moved to another comfortable bed and another set of clean bedsheets. She sat at the porthole window, listening to music, until the sun dipped to the horizon in a splendor of indigoes and pinks.

She'd always found it a mystery that humans loved to watch the sunset. It signaled the coming of darkness, the time that awakened predators and nightmares. But she too loved it. She too kept her eyes on the sun while it sank to a sliver of gold and then to nothing. She was asleep before the darkness came.

NINE

S HE COULDN'T WAIT TO RIDE TO THE BOATHOUSE she'd spotted yesterday from the beach.

After breakfast — bottled cappuccino and a slice of *halwa* topped with orange marmalade — she rode to the far end of the cove, where she found the unexpected gift of well-kept kayaks and paddles. Without wasting a moment, she grabbed a paddle, pushed one of the kayaks to the low surf and slipped into the cockpit.

Before the plague, she'd often gone kayaking alone; she loved it even more than hiking alone. Being again free from the land filled her whole being with a rush of elation she thought she was no longer capable of feeling. From the sea, the world seemed unchanged; there could have been people, only not visible. The silence was the same, that thick quiet that sometimes made her want to scream just so she could shatter it.

She followed closely the curving shoreline. Had she not been alone, she would have pushed out as far as she could. In the world of the machines, when help arrived at the pressing of a button, it had been easy to forget that being alone meant being in danger.

She kept trying to see if she could spot signs of life around or below her, but it was like looking down a dark, empty aquarium. The kelp floating by the kayak could have been drifting since long before the plague. No, nothing here either — only the paddle splashing and her breath following its rhythmic motions. But the moment was good, and she would take the moment.

She lost track of time sliding on the flat blue water. The sun warmed her naked body, and the soft wind cooled her sweat. Only hunger made her return ashore. After leaving the kayak at the boathouse, she bicycled back to the hotel and headed for the kitchen pantry.

This time she chose oysters, crab, butter biscuits and rosemary grissini to be dipped in flavored olive oil. Then she made a salad with hearts of palm, artichokes, baby corn and water chestnuts. For dessert, she picked cherries in cognac and dark chocolate thins. She opened the can of oysters on the spot, arranged the juicy mollusks on a plate and sprinkled on them some dried mint. It was an unusual seasoning preferred by her sister-in-law, from whom she'd learned many favorite recipes.

After pushing the cart to her new cottage, she ate sitting by the window, singing along with the songs on the music player. She was pleasantly exhausted after the long kayak ride, and appetite made everything tastier.

She spent the rest of the day sunbathing and reading. She waited to go swimming until sunset, when the light shifted low and made the world so mysteriously different. She'd never swum with nothing between her skin and the water; it made her smile to think that once she would have had to look for a place specially designated for the shedding of one's clothes in public. She went to bed anticipating her next day in that place of comfort and freedom. She thought of home, wondering whether she missed it. No, she didn't miss it — not yet.

A sharp pain in her stomach awakened her in the middle of the night. She sat up, dizzy and hot with fever. Her thoughts raced in every direction.

The plague had no symptoms; people were alive one instant and dead the next. And even if these were plague symptoms, why would they manifest now? There were no living humans, animals, viruses or bacteria left to infect her. Perhaps she was a carrier and didn't know it? Were there dormant germs in these places she'd never been before? Was something from the pantry contaminated? All sorts of terrifying possibilities came to her mind while she lay in the dark.

Soon her thirst became unbearable. She pulled herself up, holding onto the nightstand, and felt for the flashlight. She made her halting way to the door, then crossed barefoot the lawn to the cobblestoned path leading to the pantry. The night air made her shiver as she walked bent over with pain.

In the pantry, she opened the first bottle of water she could reach, took a long sip, retched, forced herself to take another sip. She loaded several bottles on the cart closest to her, moving slowly so she wouldn't drop them. Then she pushed the cart to her cottage, step after weary step, and collapsed on the bed without breath.

Dawn came after the longest time she'd ever waited. It didn't bring an improvement, but at least she wouldn't have to stumble around in the wobbling beam of the flashlight. She lay on the bed, watching the light from the windows change with agonizing slowness. There was nothing worse than being forced to inaction when effort was needed; it went against everything the human race had been designed to do. She could do nothing but wait, as she had waited those seven long days before she'd been condemned to solitary confinement.

She knew the old platitude that everyone dies alone. She'd been forced to make her peace with the fact that she would die doubly alone. That wasn't what saddened her. It was the thought of dying away from her life — her books, her mug, her photographs, her print, her little bird made of real bird feathers. But if this was her time, she would not die begging to be spared. She thought of the old image of Death, a faceless figure cloaked in black.

"Ready when you are, witch," she whispered.

Without a watch, she couldn't count the hours. It was long hours of pain, occupied with nothing but hoping the pain would pass. There was no shelter from her own thoughts.

How had her loved ones waited to die? she wondered. Which of them had died first? What had been *their* thoughts? Had they found the time to accept their death, or had they given in to despair? The only comfort was knowing that she could not have found out even if they had died before her eyes: in the end, they too had died alone.

At nightfall she asked herself whether she should take more of the sleep drug. She'd never done it; if one tablet induced nightmares, who knows what more than one would do. No, she decided, she couldn't risk it. She took the usual dose, and a few minutes later she was surprised to find that the drug was also a powerful painkiller. She'd never thought she'd be so thankful for something she so resented.

She woke up at first light, after a reasonable stretch of undisturbed sleep. The pain in her stomach was still strong, but the dizziness had gone down and she wasn't as feverish as before. She resigned herself to another day of misery, but not in a cage.

She walked out to the lawn chair under the palm tree, pushed the backrest all the way down and settled in comfortably. Then she closed her eyes and freed her mind to the voice of the waves alone.

By sundown she was well enough to be hungry. She crumbled two nutrition bars into a glass of water and ate them one tablespoon at a time. She would have liked to stay outside, but it was getting cold. She went back to bed, took a sleep tablet and slept soundly.

Another dawn. The dizziness had abated; she could now walk around without having to hold onto the walls. She went to check the beacon; resuming her familiar ritual gave her hope that she would soon be taking back the reins of her life. She would stay one more day in the cottage, and if the next morning the dizziness subsided enough for safe riding, she would set out for home.

She ate two more nutrition bars crumbled in water, got her music player and went to sit on the lawn chair under the palm tree. It had been a long time since she'd been up at dawn. She'd forgotten how spellbinding it was to watch the sun return and make the world new again. She found pleasure in music now, and that made time pass faster.

She didn't want to sleep again in rumpled sheets drenched with sweat. Before nighttime, she walked to the cottage closest to hers, moved everything there and set the beacon by the front door. Again, the drug gave her a night of dreamless, uninterrupted rest.

Another dawn. Its first rays came in gloriously tinged by the stained-glass windows. She spent most of the day outside, on the plush lawn chair. The pain in her stomach was still there, but if it stayed as it was, it was mild enough to allow her to ride. Only one thought occupied her mind now: home.

This time she would have to save her strength, and make at least one stop along the way. She remembered a small town just off the north entrance to the old bridge. She was reasonably sure she could reach it in one ride. She had to: there were no other sources of provisions between the Blue Cove and the town.

She turned the beacon off and packed it with the rest of her things. She made one last trip to the restaurant pantry, to get a bottle of water for her backpack. She took also one of the pretty napkin rings shaped like a nautilus shell. As she was about to leave, she went back in and took another ring. Perhaps someday someone would dine with her.

Then she bid goodbye to the Blue Cove, unsure whether she would remember her stay fondly or not. She would never know what had made her sick, and she would never know whether the sickness would come back; but she knew that it wasn't the plague, and that if it ever came back, it would pass.

She reached the old bridge speedily enough, then left the coast road and rode into the small town. It was a lovely little town; what made it lovely was that it had no hotels to spoil the stunning views and quaint narrow streets. The only hotel she could see was a long way up on the mountainside.

The weather had turned; it would start raining soon. She must find shelter in a house. She stopped at the closest one, found the door unlocked and went in. The house was in shambles: objects scattered and broken, drawers ripped from the furniture and emptied. Mixed with the dust and grime that covered everything was a layer of grey flecks. She'd been in many empty houses, but it was clear that in this one people had been murdered. She ran out, jumped on her bicycle and rode around in a panic.

She spotted a house with a *For Sale* sign. That meant the house was clean, but there was no knowing what she would find inside; and even if it was clean, it didn't have a bed. She chided herself for the stupid mistake of not bringing her sleeping bag. Raindrops were starting to fall; she heard a distant clap of thunder.

She took her chances with the first house that looked decent enough, praying the door would not be locked. The door was not locked.

It was a good place. There was dust, but other than that, everything was tidy. A woman had lived there, one who had treated herself well: a white silk blouse on her bedroom armchair, a locket enameled with initials on her dresser, a bottle of fine perfume on her vanity.

She took the beacon from her backpack, turned it on and left it by the front door, next to her bicycle. She was exhausted and thirsty. In the refrigerator, now just another cupboard but thankfully without mold, she found covered dishes containing what looked like cooked foods long gone bad, and two large bottles of water. One of the bottles was open and undrinkable, the other still sealed. She sighed with relief; the last thing she wanted was have to go outside to hunt for water.

On the kitchen shelves she found an unopened jar of preserves, a bag of chocolate wafers and a box of puff pastries, all from a country she couldn't place by the language on the containers. She wolfed down the chocolate wafers, half the jar of preserves and half the box of pastries. She'd never had any of those sweets, and she didn't know precisely what their ingredients were, but they tasted fresh and they were delicious. Nothing like sweets to mend the world sometimes, she thought. She slept well in the clean bed, under a pink satin comforter.

When she woke up, the rain had stopped. She ate a nutrition bar and what remained of the sweets, slathering jam on the pastries, then took a look around the house. She couldn't wait to go home, but she didn't want to ride on the slick roads. Better to wait a bit.

Her hostess had a collection of handsome, leather-bound books in two languages, one of them the same language that was on the packages of sweets. She picked a book written in her own language, sat in the armchair in the bright morning light, and started reading. She liked the first pages, and would have loved to read the rest. Surely, she thought, her hostess would not have minded if she took the book. She put it in one of the bicycle's saddlebags, along with the beacon, then closed the door.

"Thank you for your hospitality, my friend."

The last few miles took all of her strength. When she saw her house from the end of the street, she almost broke down in tears. Nothing in the world like home, even when home was empty.

She tossed the backpack on the living-room floor and took a long drink of water from her white and gold mug. She smiled to the little bird perched atop the zinnia.

"Hello, beauty. Did you miss me?"

She was too exhausted to eat. All she wanted was a good night's rest. She took the sleep tablet and stretched under the blanket with a deep sigh of contentment. For a drowsy moment she wondered whether survival was an option that humans chose, or simply a reflex imposed upon the species because life demanded that the species continue. Then she fell asleep.

Out by the front door, the red arc of the beacon merged with the hues of the twilight.

TEN

F OR THE FIRST FEW DAYS AFTER SHE RETURNED HOME, she thought she would never leave it again.

It rained during those days, but she had everything she needed; she wouldn't have to ride out to get provisions. It was good to sleep in her own bed again, to hear the thunder and to know she was safe. As soon as the weather cleared, she returned to her work of mowing the lawn, trimming the bushes and weeding the grass.

That afternoon she was pruning the hedges at the sides of the front door. She remembered the pretty topiaries at the Blue Cove, wishing she could make one, then laughed.

"Most likely a green blob."

The sea and the sky were an almost seamless breadth of blue. There was not a cloud on the horizon, and only the softest breeze blew. She wiped her forehead and reached for her bottle of water. Out of the corner of her eye, she caught a shape on the horizon. She shielded her face against the sun; her shears fell to the ground.

An aircraft. Not a trick of the light but a solid object, having length and girth and a shimmer of silver-grey metal, an unknown mesh of familiar and alien, a hot-air balloon with a long saucer in place of the basket. She was too astonished to make a sound.

No point in trying to flag the aircraft. If it had a crew, it was too far for them to see her. But it was not too far for them to see the beacon; and if they had seen the beacon, any moment now they would turn toward her. She could only stand still and watch.

"Turn," she whispered. "Turn."

The aircraft kept gliding silently, its metallic glint flickering in the sunlight. It followed a steady southward course, at a speed low enough for her to keep her eyes fixed on it while it moved smoothly in the sky. The more she looked at it, the more she knew it was real.

She shook herself from her amazement, ran into the house, searched for her binoculars, found them and dashed out again. The aircraft was still there, but now all she could make out through the binoculars' lenses was the silver-grey flicker, floating away until it could be seen no more.

She breathed in hard. "All right, all right ... Think."

She went back into the house and got the video camera, careful not to let it slip from her unsteady hands. Then she took the tripod, placed it on the laneway in front of the lawn, turned the camera on and set it to continuous mode and 180 degrees rotation.

"What else, what else ...? An SOS sign? And how would that improve on the beacon, you dimwit?"

She paced around, moving her hands to calm herself.

"All right, all right."

She sat on the patio all day, and then well past sundown, unable to eat or do anything else. Everything had changed. She didn't know where to start rearranging the pieces. A host of conjectures crowded her mind. She forced herself to consider them one at a time, rationally if she could.

Was it a manned aircraft, and if so, why hadn't they noticed the beacon? Was it an unmanned drone, and if so, had it alerted rescuers? And the one question she could have never have imagined: was the aircraft human?

She scoffed at herself. To her, the idea that other sentient beings lived in other corners of the universe had always been wishful thinking, a childish refusal on the part of humans to accept that they were orphans. There was no proof; belief was not fact. Endless variations of the fairytale had taken root in the collective imagination; and the trouble with humans, someone had once said, was that they could imagine everything.

She would not give in to wishful thinking now. So this aircraft was unlike any she'd ever seen. That didn't mean it was not human; it meant it was a kind of human aircraft unlike any she'd ever seen. Who knows what had happened outside her speck of the world since she'd last heard from the rest of the world?

The stars were out. The air had cooled enough to make her shiver. Sleep was the last thing she wanted, but without sleep she knew she wouldn't be able to face whatever came next. She told herself she must start learning the patience to wait for things to happen without her intervention. One could go mad from hope as easily as from despair.

She wondered whether she should leave the door open, so she could be more quickly found. No, she thought then. From this day on, she would again have to worry about what might come in through the door. She locked all the doors, lowered all the blinds, drew all the drapes and turned off all the lights. Before taking the sleep drug, she went to look out the window one last time; then she surrendered to sleep.

Outside, the only thing moving in the night was the pulse of the beacon.

*   *   *

The plague came from beings not human, they'd spared her as an experiment, they were watching her from the aircraft, she would never be rescued.

The thought burst into her mind the moment she woke up. She could not dismiss it as absurd; her whole existence had became a chain of absurdities. This too must be brought into the new territory of the possible.

Long ago she had chosen to be faithful to herself, and that was all she could do. A fundamental numbness was needed, a buffer between her and the nightmare that life was asking her to survive. She would find it.

She took a deep breath, put on her slippers and went to check the beacon. The beacon pulsed and the sky was empty. She closed the door and went to make breakfast.

ELEVEN

SOMETHING WAS CALLING HER BACK TO THE LIBRARY. Since the day she'd remained alone, she'd avoided even riding past it. It didn't take her much imagination to know what the library had become: a dark, littered place inhabited only by the words of the dead.

The worst was remembering the children. They had come in happy, eager swarms, dressed in every color of the rainbow. They had sat on the floor, listening in rapt silence or laughing or clapping their hands, while she read them the stories and showed them the pictures.

She'd never understood how some people could be annoyed by children, how they could dislike their high voices and boisterous laughter. She delighted in children's gleeful disregard for the rules, the lovely freedom that would have to be stripped from them too soon. Sometimes she shushed them only because she was expected to do it.

The death of children had always seemed to her the most illogical of evolution's rules, Earth destroying its own future. And nothing pained her more than knowing she would never have children of her own.

Finally, she made up her mind. She told herself she would be strong; she must be strong. She took her bicycle and rode up the steep, narrow street she'd taken almost every day of her life for over seven years. The door of the library was unlocked. If it had been locked, she was ready to smash the glass with a rock. She turned her flashlight on and stepped inside.

She could have found her way around with her eyes closed. It was *her* library; it had been entrusted to her, and she had taken good care of it for over seven years. She knew where everything was: the book shelves, the music shelves, the video shelves, the computers, the printers, the donation compartment, the copy machine, the reading booths, the newspaper racks, the magazine racks, the lost-and-found bin, the pencil holders.

She stood in the middle of the vast interior, looking at the desolation and wondering what she wanted to do. The world was in shambles, but here it seemed more of an offense. This was a place predicated upon order — things painstakingly sorted, labeled, numbered, catalogued and placed in their assigned space.

She picked up a book from the floor and read the tag at the bottom of the spine.

"Natural Sciences, C-H."

Almost unconsciously, she searched for the section where the book belonged. She found the shelf, slipped the book into its assigned space and straightened up the row. How familiar those gestures were; they had never seemed repetitive.

She picked up another book, found the shelf where it belonged, slipped it into its assigned space and straightened up the row. Then she picked up an armful of books and, one by one, put them back in the place where they belonged. She lost track of time; if she hadn't glanced at the door, she would have never noticed it was almost sundown.

She looked at the two long shelves she had restored, and nodded.

"If you have all the time in the world, use it."

From that day on, she went back to the library every day. She restocked shelves, wiped dust away, cleared out rubbish, scrubbed rust clean, rearranged desks, tacked posters back to the walls. Little by little, the smell of decay was replaced by the scent of cleaning liquids, and the stuffy air became fresh again from the open windows.

She worked until her every muscle ached and she barely had energy left to ride home. It was a good kind of fatigue; it came from doing something she wanted to do, instead of something she had to do. Perhaps no one else would ever return to her library, but while she had the strength, she would keep the place where she had worked as tidy as she kept the place where she lived.

Only with the children's room did she keep procrastinating. On the floor were a pink umbrella and two small backpacks, and she didn't want to go near them. Her little nephew had started school some months before the plague, and had carried a backpack like those.

It took all her willpower to restore the children's room. She cleaned up the litter, straightened the bookshelves, stowed the toys in the toy bin and arranged the small chairs around the table, as she had done every time the children had come to hear the stories. Last, she tucked into a cubbyhole the pink umbrella and the two small backpacks. She stroked them gently, then granted herself the luxury of sobs that made her soul feel cleaner too.

Before going home, she looked back at the library and she thought of the accumulated centuries of human experience that books preserved: the unspeakable, the mundane, the sublime. In the back of her mind was always the fear that the silver-grey aircraft was not human, and that she was the unwilling subject of an experiment by beings that didn't have the civility to reveal themselves.

"What are you trying to discover?" she addressed them in a whisper. "Let me save you the work. Humans are the ultimate mystery. There is nothing they won't do to each other, and there is nothing they won't do for each other. That is all you need to know about us. Go home."

*   *   *

The water was boiling. She opened the canister decorated with blooming poppies in which she kept the teabags, then took her white and gold mug from the cupboard.

On the rim of the mug she noticed a large chip that had almost obliterated the name of her alma mater. She didn't remember how the chip had happened; the mug was one of the things she treated with the most care. She felt a surge of anger: how could she have been so stupid?

She dropped the teabag into a plastic cup instead, poured hot water in and went to sit on the rocking chair by the window. Out on the horizon, she could see bright gold shafts knifing from the clouds to the sea. She didn't have to ride today; it would be a good day for working in the backyard.

From behind the pine trees, the silver-grey aircraft glided silently toward her. She let go of the cup, jumping out of her chair. She rushed to the front door, slammed it open: no signs of the aircraft.

As she awoke with a start, it took her a moment to orient herself. She was sitting on the sofa, with one of the cushions propped up behind her head; she'd fallen asleep in the middle of the day. It didn't happen often, but she'd spent the morning working hard on the overgrown myrtles in the backyard. She must have been more tired than she thought.

She was annoyed rather than upset by the dream. It was simply her mind reliving the elation and heartache of the aircraft arriving and departing. She went to the kitchen and made tea. When she took the white and gold mug from the cupboard, she was not surprised to see its rim wasn't chipped.

She finished her tea, then went to check the video camera by the front lawn. It was a ritual no less unnecessary than checking the beacon; the video camera alerted her as soon as it detected movement. She was not surprised to see there had been no movement.

She returned to the kitchen, washed the mug and dried it. She thought of the dream, shaking her head in deep irritation.

"Making Sigmund proud," she muttered.

She put on her gardening gloves and returned to the myrtles.

She was forced to stop sooner than she wanted. A storm had come up from the sea while she was engrossed in her work. It lashed the coast with thunder and lightning all night. Once or twice, she heard branches crashing outside, not too close to the house. It didn't seem alarming enough for her to venture outside in the pouring rain; it wasn't the first time a storm tore branches off the trees.

The sun was back the following morning. She missed hearing birdsong when she opened the windows. Who knows what birds had said to each other, in their languages as wonderfully varied as human languages. What birds had said to each other had sometimes sounded to her more beautiful than any human love song.

When she went to check the beacon, she was aghast to see it lay smashed under a branch that had fallen off the pine tree next to the patio. For all she knew, the beacon had stopped working the moment she'd closed the door before going to bed; that was a long time to be invisible. She damned herself for not going out when she'd heard the first crashing sounds. If the beacon had been smashed then, she could have replaced it immediately with the spare.

Too upset to walk the usual distance from the house, she tossed the broken beacon off the cliff from her front door. Then, without eating breakfast, she made the long trek to the store to get a new spare beacon. While she pedaled hard, she looked up at the sky; if there were watchers in the aircraft, she thought, she must look no different to them than an ant scuttling after crumbs.

TWELVE

T HE WEATHER WAS PLEASANT ENOUGH TO GO SWIMMING.
She stuffed her sunhat and a bath towel in a canvas bag and
headed for the wooden staircase that led down to the beach.

The staircase had exactly two hundred and sixteen steps;
she'd counted them the first time she'd climbed them with her
mother. Her mother, who'd carried extra pounds, had joked that
climbing those two hundred and sixteen steps again would be
the death of her.

She took off her sandals, to feel again the warm weathered
wood of the staircase under her feet. The sun was sweet on her
face; the waves washed over the pale sand with long, murmuring
strokes. If humans didn't find the world half beautiful, she
thought, they couldn't find it half bearable. She felt an unexpected

sense of peace, the long-forgotten difference between loneliness and solitude.

Her favorite swimming spot was the small cove to the north. The water was calmer there; the curving arms of the rock sheltered it from the wind. She went down the last step and walked toward the cove. Her gaze swept across the surface of the sea. It was as it had always been, but there was so much humans had never found out about the depths, and would have never found out even if they had survived.

The water was a bit cooler than she remembered. It was a pleasant kind of coolness, that enlivened her and made her swim more vigorously. She pushed out as far as she judged safe for her to return to shore without tiring herself too much.

Something stirred on the horizon, making her stop. At first she thought it was a taller wave. It could be nothing else; for months, the only thing she'd seen moving on the water were waves. An instant later, she realized it *was* something else: two graceful shapes with fins and tails, leaping up, arching high in the air, plunging back, leaping up, plunging back — the plain and simple shapes of two dolphins.

"That's impossible," she whispered.

The sun shone brightly behind the two shapes, making their outlines sharp and clear. It was not an illusion; it was two living creatures, alive and healthy. She laughed to the sky, waving her arms.

"Hey! Hey! Hello!"

The dolphins leapt and splashed, making the water foam with their strong, lithe bodies that mirrored each other's movements.

"Oh you beautiful things! Come closer, can you see me? Come closer!"

She couldn't remember when she'd felt such joy, and such frustration. They were too far for her to swim to them, and she didn't have a boat. She floated on the spot, transfixed. She knew they wouldn't come to her, but she kept calling out and waving her arms, while they danced in the waves.

Now they were moving away. She could see the shape of their fins changing into the shape of their tails.

"No, no! Stay, please stay!"

With one last leap, they disappeared.

She kept floating until her arms and legs were sore, but they were gone — for now.

For now.

The words she had exchanged with her parents when everything was lost were true again. The sea was not a desert. It was a treasure house of things strange and marvelous. For every wonder it concealed, it revealed another.

To think that these lovely creatures, and so many others, had almost been killed off. Humans had swarmed everywhere, depredated everything, to feed their unsustainable numbers. Perhaps, she thought, the plague had been the Earth's way of saving herself from beings who thought they were her masters.

She swam ashore and climbed the staircase, much quicker than she'd climbed it down, then ran to check the video camera. Yes, the camera had captured the dolphins' dance; she could be sure it hadn't been a dream. She watched the video again and again, clapping her hands like a little girl. She now had two things to scan for, she thought; but while she didn't know whether the aircraft meant salvation or fear, the dolphins were pure hope.

From the top of the bluff, she looked back one last time, then went in and closed the door.

THIRTEEN

IT HAD TAKEN HER WEEKS to reach her parents' house. She'd ridden in good weather and bad, made dozens of stops along the way, wondering all along the way whether she really wanted to see the house again. Now she was standing on its front steps.

The house was untouched. Everything was as she remembered: the old swing where she and her brother had played when they were little, her mother's plump hydrangeas in the window boxes, her father's well-used toolkit by the fencepost. The only thing reminding her that the house was empty was the pile of yellowed newspapers on the stoop.

While she lingered, yearning to go inside and yet dreading to see what was inside, she heard a sound that seemed familiar, though she couldn't tell where she'd heard it before. She looked around, then raised her head: the silver-grey aircraft was hovering behind the house, low enough for her to see shapes standing at the portholes.

Before she had time to choose between relief and terror, the aircraft landed with a soft whirring sound. Its door opened. A figure emerged. She couldn't see it clearly, but she was instantly aware that it was not human, and that it had not come to save her. She pounded her fists on the door of the house, knowing the house would not protect her but not knowing where else to go. She woke up to the sound of her own scream.

The rest of the day was nothing but daze. She wandered around as if something had hit her in the belly, gasping for air and muttering nonsense. She understood that the aircraft would return in her nightmares again and again: it was embedded in her soul. It would blur reality and illusion again and again, wrench her from one deception to the other again and again, and in the end it would consume her. For all she knew, that was the experiment she'd been singled out for, by whoever was watching her from the aircraft. She was as good as dead.

Only later she forced herself to go to the backyard, and cut and slash until her arms hurt and the hedges were reduced to ragged stumps. She could not eat, she could not read, music would have been salt in the wounds. She told herself she would never take the sleep drug again. She could not stand the thought of being leashed to whatever detested and indispensable substance was inside that little white tablet.

But sleep would not come. At the end of her endurance, she thought even another nightmare was better than wandering around the house in a daze. She dragged herself to the medicine cabinet and swallowed the little white tablet. She didn't know what to curse anymore: the drug, her weakness, life itself. She went back to bed, then finally felt the approaching mercy of oblivion, praying she would never wake up.

Nothing stirred outside but the high arc of the beacon.

FOURTEEN

MANY WEEKS PASSED, remembered as nothing more than box after box crossed out on her calendar.

At first, more than ever, there was nothing tethering her to the world. She had nothing to prove to others by staying alive. If she gave up, there was no one to call her a coward, and she was not sure she cared anymore if she called herself a coward. Sometimes, without taking the sleep drug, she slept through the day too, so she could escape herself.

Yet, after those first dreadful days, she again rose every day, and every day she found something to do, even when it was like digging and filling and digging the same ditch. She didn't know from where the strength came to dig and fill and dig. She did what she had to do, and she did what she wanted to do. She checked her beacon, brought home her necessities, cleaned her house and tended her lawn.

As she had promised herself many times, she went to every store within her reach and took home nothing but non-essentials — the non-essentials that were in fact essential, because humans had always prized beauty: an antique silver frame for her print, a wreath of red silk berries for her front door, a hand-embroidered cushion for her rocking chair. She fought defeat even in the small things, as when she ate out of a plate instead of out of a can. The word "instead" was what kept her breathing now.

"We love you, darling. Stay strong."

One afternoon, the video camera flashed. It was the dolphins, playing again in the sunlight at the far end of the cove, like beloved kinfolk returning to call on her. She watched them ecstatically, forgetting everything else.

Often she chose to go to the library and read there, in the beam of her flashlight. She loved the familiar smell of the place: aging paper, pencil lead, ink. It was the time that flew faster and never dulled. Those who had written the books would have never imagined that someday there would be only one reader; but she knew that while she read their words, their words lived. Each book was a world. There was so much to learn.

She thought of the silver-grey aircraft only when she went to check the beacon and the video camera. It had taken her a long time, but in the end she had learned to push it into a corner of her mind. It was either that or letting it destroy her. The greatest temptation was to stop counting the days, to let time swallow her into a hazy pit of unnumbered sunrises and sunsets. She did not stop counting the days.

Then, one morning, her calendar said it was the first day of spring. She already knew it; spring to her was now the way the air felt, the way the wind moved. That morning she rose, checked the beacon and the video camera, washed up and ate breakfast. Then she stood at her bookcase and chose a book. She had removed all the photographs from the shelves. Someday, when it no longer hurt, she would put them back.

She went to the patio and sat under the dappled shade of the pine trees. The sea was a calm sweep gleaming in the afternoon sun. The days were getting longer, the light bolder. Winter had passed, and she had survived it. Perhaps it was enough.

She thought of the dolphins playing in the cove, their sleek arching bodies mirroring each other's movements in their lovely dance. She knew why she could never be away from the sea. The sea was vast and full of secrets. It was the birthplace of life, and it had guarded life. If two of the species had survived, more had survived, and if their species had survived, more species had survived. She was not the sole custodian of the planet.

She sat down and opened her book. It was a birthday gift from her father, when she was much younger. Inside, he had written a quotation by one of his favorite writers: "Books talk even when they're closed. Blessed are those who can hear their whispering voices." She moved the bookmark to another page and started reading.

Some time later, she heard a sound that reminded her of a crow faintly cawing in the distance. She looked up: it was the silver-grey aircraft, as real as she'd seen it the first time, closer than she'd seen it the first time, and this time headed toward her. She could barely breathe while she watched it float over the bluff, then hover above the trees, then land with a soft whirring sound.

The whirring died down. The door of the aircraft opened. Two arms emerged, then another two, then two legs, then another two, then two faces.

Human.

She heard them call her by her name. She rose and went to greet them, with her book in her hand.

ABOUT THE AUTHOR

Flavia Idà was born and raised in Italy. She studied the classics and modern literature at the University of Naples. Flavia is also a language teacher, translator, and freelance journalist with pieces published in English and Italian. She lives in Pacifica, California. Find out more about Flavia's works and world at *Flavia's Voice* (flaviasvoice.com)

YOU MIGHT ALSO ENJOY

THE IRON AND THE LOOM
A Novel of Italy

by Flavia Idà

How many times, she wondered, had she woven together cloth that his sword had then torn apart along with the flesh underneath?

THE NAMES OF HEAVEN
by Flavia Idà

One man. An extraordinary choice.

CHILDREN OF THE WRONG TIME
by Flavia Idà

"Would you say you were loved by the right people at the right time in the right way and for the right reasons?"

www.ingramcontent.com/pod-product-compliance
Lightning Source LLC
Chambersburg PA
CBHW020640130626
46552CB00003B/1327